THE WALTZ OF ECSTASY

A SHORT, EROTIC, REGENCY-ERA STORY

ELIZA FINCH

1

The moon cast its silvery glow upon the elegant ballroom, illuminating the grandeur of the high arched ceilings adorned with intricate gold-leaf designs. Flickering candlelight from opulent chandeliers danced across the polished marble floors, reflecting off the faces of the elite guests in attendance. The soft strains of a string quartet filled the air, weaving a seductive melody that entwined with the whispers and laughter of the revelers.

Amidst the sea of swirling gowns and tailored suits, Amelia stood out like a beacon of sensuality. The young widow's gown clung to her voluptuous curves like a lover's embrace, the rich fabric shimmering with each subtle movement. Her eyes were pools of longing, brimming with unfulfilled passion and the promise of forbidden romance. She moved through the crowd with an air of quiet confidence, her gaze occasionally lingering on the handsome gentlemen who approached her, their desires laid bare before her discerning eyes.

"Forgive my boldness, but I couldn't help but notice you from across the room," a suave voice murmured near Amelia's ear, sending shivers down her spine. Turning towards the source of the voice, she found herself face-to-face with a devilishly handsome man whose gaze seemed to penetrate her very soul.

"Is that so?" Amelia replied coyly, her voice dripping with intrigue. "And what is it about me that has captured your attention?"

"Ah, where do I begin?" the stranger mused, his eyes roving over her body with unabashed appreciation. "Your beauty, of course, is undeniable. But there's something more... a fire burning within you, begging to be unleashed."

"Careful," Amelia warned playfully, her eyes narrowing as a sultry smile graced her lips. "You're dangerously close to discovering my deepest secrets."

"Perhaps that's precisely what I want," he countered, his voice low and husky as he leaned in closer. "To explore every inch of you, and uncover your hidden desires."

"Is that a promise or a threat?" Amelia breathed, feeling her pulse quicken under the weight of his gaze.

"Both," he replied with a wicked grin. "And I assure you, my dear, I fully intend to keep it."

As they continued their dance of words, each exchange filled with innuendo and unspoken lust, Amelia found herself drawn further into the magnetic pull of this enigmatic stranger. And despite her better judgment, she couldn't help but wonder if this was the man who could finally satisfy the hunger that had been gnawing at her for so long.

As the moonlight filtered through the grand windows of the ballroom, casting an ethereal glow upon the dancers below, Lord Alexander made his entrance. The charismatic aristocrat moved effortlessly through the crowd, his mischievous smile and piercing eyes causing hearts to flutter and cheeks to redden with every stolen glance. There was something undeniably magnetic about him, an aura that seemed to envelop those in his presence, leaving them entranced and yearning for more.

"Ah, Amelia," he purred as he approached her, his voice like velvet slipping over her skin. "You look ravishing tonight."

"Lord Alexander," she replied breathlessly, her pulse quickening at the sight of him. She could feel the weight of his gaze on her body, as though he were undressing her with his eyes.

"May I have this dance?" he asked, extending a hand to her. With a sultry smile, Amelia placed her hand in his, allowing him to lead her onto the dance floor.

As they began to move together, their bodies in perfect harmony, Amelia found herself lost in the rhythm of the music and the heat of Alexander's touch. His fingers traced delicate patterns along the small of her back, sending shivers down her spine. The intoxicating scent of his cologne filled her senses, making her head swim with desire.

"Your dancing is exquisite, my dear," Alexander whispered into her ear, his hot breath fanning across her neck.

"Thank you," she murmured, her voice barely audible above the pounding of her heart.

In one swift motion, Amelia stepped forward, her foot landing squarely on Alexander's toes. They both stumbled, their bodies pressed tightly against each other as they tried to regain their balance. The sudden contact sent a jolt of electricity through them, igniting a fire within that neither could ignore.

"Apologies, my lord," Amelia stammered, her cheeks flushed with embarrassment.

"Think nothing of it," he replied, his voice husky with desire. "After all, accidents can lead to the most... delightful surprises."

Their eyes locked, an unspoken invitation passing between them as they resumed their dance. The sensual, evocative language of their bodies spoke louder than any words could – a steamy, erotic atmosphere enveloping them as they moved together in perfect sync.

"Tell me, Amelia," Alexander murmured as his lips brushed against her earlobe, causing her to shiver with anticipation. "What secret fantasies do you harbor deep within?"

"Yours is not a privilege to know," she shot back playfully, biting her lower lip seductively.

"Ah, but that only makes me want it more," he replied with a wicked grin, his hand slipping down to cup the swell of her hip. "I have a feeling we'd make quite the scandalous pair."

"Is that so?" Amelia asked breathlessly, her body responding to his bold advances despite her mind's protests.

"Indeed," Alexander whispered, his fingers tracing a tantalizing path up her thigh. "But I think you'll find my appetite for sin insatiable."

"Be careful what you wish for, my lord," Amelia warned, her voice sultry and laced with promise. "You just might get it."

The warm scent of Amelia's perfume mingled with the faint aroma of candle wax as they danced, their bodies pressed close together. The lingering touch of Alexander's hand on her waist sent a jolt of electricity through her, igniting a fire deep within her core.

"Amelia," Alexander whispered huskily, his breath hot against her earlobe. "I can't help but feel our connection is... magnetic."

"Is that so?" she replied, allowing her fingers to trail suggestively along the nape of his neck. "You're quite daring, Lord Alexander."

"Life's too short for anything less than passion and desire," he murmured, his eyes darkening with lust. "Which begs the question, what do you truly crave?"

Amelia bit her lip, her heart pounding in her chest as she leaned in closer to him, her voice low and seductive. "I think you'll find I'm not as innocent as I appear, my lord."

"Ah," Alexander said, grinning wickedly as his hand dipped lower, gripping her ass firmly. "You've piqued my interest, Amelia. Perhaps we can explore these hidden desires together?"

"Perhaps," she whispered, her breath hitching as she felt his arousal pressing against her thigh. "But only if you can keep up with me."

"Challenge accepted," Alexander growled, his other hand sliding up her back to pull her even tighter against him. "I have a feeling this will be a night neither of us will forget."

As their bodies moved in perfect harmony to the sultry rhythm of the music, the rest of the world seemed to fade away, leaving only the intoxicating allure of their shared desire. Their heated gazes never strayed from one another, revealing the depths of their unbridled passion and the promise of an erotic journey that lay just beyond their reach.

The moonlit ballroom was a whirl of glittering gowns and dashing gentlemen, but for Amelia and Lord Alexander, it was as if they were the only two people in the room. Their breaths mingled, their bodies swaying to the seductive beat of the music as they moved ever closer to one another.

"Your hand is awfully close to my bosom, my lord," Amelia whispered, her cheeks flushing with a rosy hue as she felt Alexander's fingers gently brushing against her. The contact sent shivers up her spine, tantalizing her senses.

"Is it now?" Alexander replied, his voice low and suggestive. He entwined their fingers together, causing Amelia's pulse to quicken. "I see no problem with that, do you?"

Her eyes widened, caught off guard by his forwardness. She hesitated, then admitted, "No, I don't."

"Good," he murmured, his lips brushing her earlobe as he spoke, making her tremble with anticipation. "We wouldn't want anything to distract us from this... intimate dance, would we?"

Amelia's shy and demure nature seemed to be at odds with

Alexander's confident and seductive demeanor. As they continued to dance, the palpable tension between them grew, creating an electrifying atmosphere that promised untamed passion.

"Have you ever been truly ravished, Amelia?" Alexander asked, his voice rough with desire. "Have you ever had your body worshipped by a man who knows exactly what you need?"

A gasp escaped her lips as she imagined the possibilities, her heart pounding in her chest. "No, I haven't," she confessed, her voice barely audible.

"Would you like me to show you what it feels like?" His words were laced with promise, sending shivers down her spine.

"Y-yes," she stammered, her gaze locked on his piercing eyes.

"Then let's see how much you can handle," Alexander growled, gripping her hand tightly as they continued their dance. With each step, Amelia felt herself being drawn closer and closer to the brink of surrender, aching to experience the erotic heights that only Lord Alexander could take her to. As the music swelled around them, so too did the sensual tension between them, leaving them both yearning for more.

Amelia's body swayed in tandem with Alexander's as they danced, their movements fluid and graceful like two feathers caught in a gentle breeze. The flaring candlelight cast flickering shadows on Amelia's flushed cheeks, amplifying the rosy hue that had blossomed there.

"Alexander," she whispered, her breath hitching as he pulled her close, the heat radiating from his muscular form enveloping her. "I feel... alive."

"Good," he replied, a wicked grin playing on his lips. "That's exactly what I want you to feel."

As they continued to dance, each stolen glance and lingering touch between them only served to stoke the fire within. Alexander's hand slid down her waist, stopping at the curve of her hip before he slyly slipped it under the folds of her gown. He squeezed her thigh gently, eliciting a sharp intake of breath from Amelia.

"Such a sweet reaction," Alexander murmured, his voice thick with lust. "I wonder what other parts of your body would respond the same way?" Amelia's heart pounded relentlessly in her chest, her thoughts racing with illicit images fueled by his provocative words.

"Y-you're so bold, Alexander," she managed to say, her voice trembling with desire.

"Boldness is necessary when one wants to experience the true depths of pleasure," he countered, his fingers continuing their tantalizing exploration up her thigh. "Tell me, Amelia, have you ever been touched like this before?"

"N-no," she stammered, her eyes wide with a mix of shock and curiosity.

"Then allow me to be the first," he said, his voice dripping with seduction, as his hand moved closer to her most intimate place. Her breath hitched in anticipation, her body trembling with need.

"Please... don't tease me," Amelia pleaded, her eyes meeting his in a silent plea for release.

"Teasing is just the beginning, my dear," Alexander replied, his fingers finally slipping between her legs. "I will make you beg for more before this night is over."

Amelia's moans filled the air as she surrendered to the pleasure Alexander expertly brought forth, their dance becoming a salacious expression of unbridled lust and desire. And as they twirled across the ballroom floor, all pretense of propriety vanished, leaving only the promise of carnal delights yet to come.

Amelia's laughter rang out like the sweetest melody, harmonizing with Alexander's deep chuckle as they shared a private joke. The intimacy of the moment cocooned them, isolating them from the bustling ballroom around them.

"Your wit is as enchanting as your beauty," Alexander whispered into her ear, his breath warm and tantalizing.

"Flattery will get you nowhere, my lord," Amelia teased, a mischievous glint in her eyes. "But please, do go on."

Alexander smirked, his fingers trailing along the exposed skin of her back, causing shivers to run down her spine. "I must admit, I find it difficult to keep my hands off you. Your body calls to me, begging to be touched, to be claimed."

"Is that so?" Amelia's voice trembled with anticipation, her heart pounding fiercely in her chest. Her mind raced with provocative images, each more daring than the last.

"Indeed," he purred, his hand dancing dangerously close to the curve of her ass. "Would you like me to demonstrate just how much I desire you?"

"Perhaps," she breathed, her eyes locked onto his.

As the music around them swelled, their bodies pressed closer together, the heat between them igniting a fire that threatened to consume them both. Amelia could feel Alexander's arousal pressing against her thigh, and the knowledge of his lust for her sent a wave of desire crashing through her.

"Your scent intoxicates me," Alexander murmured, his nose grazing her neck. "I want to taste every inch of you, to savor the flavor of your passion."

"Your words are sinful, Alexander," she replied, a blush creeping up her cheeks, yet unable to resist the allure of his erotic promises.

"Sinful, perhaps, but honest," he countered, his fingertips brushing against her erect nipple through the thin fabric of her gown. "Tell me, Amelia, do you crave my touch as much as I crave yours?"

His words hung heavy between them, an unspoken temptation that demanded an answer. And as the dance floor seemed to fade away, leaving only their shared world of desire, Amelia knew there was no turning back.

"More than you can imagine," she whispered, surrendering to the passion that burned within her.

The echoes of their laughter still lingered in the air, a shared secret that bound them closer together than any physical touch. Amelia's heart raced as she gazed into Alexander's intensely passionate eyes, her breath catching in her throat. The melting boundaries between their bodies left no space for secrets, as their desires became one.

"Amelia," Alexander breathed, his voice thick with lust, "I want to take you somewhere more... private."

"Show me," Amelia whispered back, an unspoken agreement laced with anticipation.

With their fingers entwined, Alexander led her through the grand doors of the ballroom and into the dimly lit corridors. The shadows danced along the walls, teasing them with glimpses of the forbidden pleasures that awaited.

"Are you sure about this?" Alexander asked, his tone a mix of seduction and concern. "Once we cross this threshold, there is no turning back."

"Alexander," Amelia purred, her voice dripping with arousal, "I have never been more certain of anything in my life. Take me, claim me as your own."

"Your wish is my command," he growled, pulling her tight against his body. Their lips crashed together like a storm, tongues dueling for dominance in a primal dance of desire.

As they stumbled into a darkened room, the door slamming shut behind them, Amelia felt her last shred of restraint shatter. The world beyond these walls ceased to exist; it was just the two of them now, encapsulated in a realm of pure carnal pleasure.

"Fuck," Alexander groaned, pushing Amelia against the wall,

his hands roaming her body with possessive urgency. "You're so goddamned irresistible."

"Take me, Alexander," she begged, her hips grinding against his erection. "I need you inside me."

"Patience, my dear," he teased, sinking to his knees before her. "I have every intention of feasting upon your sweet, wet pussy before I fuck you into oblivion."

As Alexander's lips met her quivering core, Amelia's mind was consumed by the overwhelming sensations that coursed through her body. She could barely form a coherent thought, let alone protest the voyeuristic gaze she felt from the shadows.

"Amelia," he groaned as he thrust his tongue deeper, "you taste like heaven and sin combined."

"Alexander," Amelia whimpered, "please, I need more."

"Your wish is my command," he growled, standing up and positioning himself at her entrance.

Before he could enter her, however, a sudden noise from the door shattered their passionate reverie. Amelia's eyes widened in horror, realizing they were no longer alone in their world of desire.

"Who's there?" Alexander demanded, shielding Amelia protectively

THE DOOR CREAKED OPEN, revealing a figure obscured by darkness, their intentions unknown. As Amelia and Alexander stared into the abyss, their hearts pounding with fear and anticipation.

"Ah, it seems we have an uninvited guest," the mysterious figure murmured, stepping closer to the light, their identity still hidden in shadow.

2

Amelia gasped, her heart pounding in her chest. She recognized the mysterious figure leaning against the doorframe – the same man who had swept her off her feet on the dance floor earlier that night.

"William," he introduced himself, his voice low and sultry. "I couldn't help but watch you two. It seems I'm not the only one who can't resist your charms, Amelia."

Amelia's cheeks burned with embarrassment, but she couldn't deny the thrill that coursed through her at his confession. She remembered the electricity between them as they danced, the way his hands had felt on her waist, guiding her movements with practiced ease.

"Is it really so surprising?" Alexander replied, a hint of cockiness slipping into his tone. "After all, we both saw how irresistible she was on that dance floor."

"Indeed," William agreed, his gaze never leaving Amelia's. "But I must admit, I'm disappointed. I thought our connection was special. To see you here, with him... it stings."

Amelia bit her lip, torn between guilt and the undeniable

arousal that sparked within her at William's words. The intensity of his gaze sent shivers down her spine, making her feel vulnerable yet powerful all at once.

"William, I... I didn't mean to hurt you," she stammered, unsure of how to navigate the situation. "It's just... I know Alexander. And there's something about Alexander that draws me in."

"Is that so?" William's eyes narrowed, a challenge simmering beneath the surface. "Well then, by all means, don't let me interrupt your passionate rendezvous."

His words dripped with sarcasm, but Amelia could sense the genuine anger beneath them. She glanced between Alexander and William, the two men who had ignited a fire within her that she hadn't known existed. As guilt and desire warred within her, Amelia knew she couldn't ignore the pull she felt towards both of them.

"Actually," William began, his voice low and steady, a wicked grin forming on his lips, "I have a proposition for you both."

Amelia's heart raced in anticipation, her fingers digging into Alexander's muscular arm. The room seemed to grow hotter, the air thick with tension.

"Go on," Alexander prompted, his curiosity piqued. His body pressed against Amelia's from behind, the heat of their skin melding together like molten lava.

"Since you two seem so eager to fuck each other's brains out," William continued, his eyes never leaving Amelia's, "I want to watch."

Amelia's breath hitched, the words sending a jolt of excitement coursing through her veins. She could feel Alexander's grip tighten around her waist, betraying his own arousal at the thought.

"Surely, you can't be serious," Amelia whispered, her cheeks flushed and pulse pounding as she met William's gaze head-on.

"Deadly serious," he replied, his voice dripping with desire.

"After all, it's only fair, isn't it? You get to have your fun, and I get to witness it. A fitting consolation prize, don't you think?"

Amelia swallowed hard, torn between shock and a growing need to indulge in this forbidden fantasy. She looked to Alexander, searching his eyes for any sign of hesitation or disapproval. But instead, she saw only raw hunger, his pupils dilated with lust.

"Fuck it," Alexander growled, his voice rough with desire. "Let him watch."

"Are you sure?" Amelia breathed, her body trembling with anticipation. "There's no turning back after this."

"Like I said, let him watch," Alexander repeated, an unmistakeable edge to his tone that left no room for doubt.

William's grin widened, his eyes locked onto Amelia's as he settled into a nearby chair. He leaned back, his hands gripping the armrests as if he were preparing for the performance of a lifetime.

"Then let the show begin," he murmured, his voice barely audible above the sound of Amelia's pounding heart.

As Amelia surrendered to the passion that coursed through her veins, she knew that this night would forever be etched into her memory, an intoxicating blend of temptation, desire, and the thrill of being watched by the very man who had ignited such raw, carnal lust within her soul.

"Touch me, Alexander," Amelia whispered, her voice trembling with urgency. He obliged, his large, calloused hands gliding over her soft skin, exploring every inch of her body as she moaned with pleasure.

"Tell me what you want, Amelia," he murmured into her ear, the heat of his breath sending shivers down her spine. She hesitated for a moment, glancing at William who was still watching intently from his chair.

"Both of you," she confessed, her cheeks flushing with embarrassment. "I want both of you to fuck me."

"Are you sure?" Alexander asked, his eyes searching hers for any sign of doubt. Amelia nodded, suddenly feeling more alive than she had ever felt before.

"Fuck her, Alexander," William commanded, his voice heavy with lust. "And don't hold back."

Alexander wasted no time, positioning himself between Amelia's thighs and thrusting inside her without warning. She cried out in ecstasy, her nails digging into his shoulders as he began to move within her.

"William, come here," Amelia panted, her body writhing beneath Alexander's powerful strokes. The other man rose from his seat, swiftly undressing before joining them on the bed.

"Where do you want me, Amelia?" William asked, his voice low and seductive.

"Inside me, too," she gasped, unable to believe the words were coming out of her mouth. William grinned wickedly, positioning himself behind her and slowly pushing his length into her tight entrance, filling her completely.

"Fuck!" Amelia screamed, her body stretched deliciously between the two men. They set a steady rhythm, their bodies moving in perfect harmony as they fucked her senseless.

"Are you enjoying this, Amelia?" William groaned, the sound of his voice dripping with desire. She could only nod, her mind awash with pleasure as both men continued to thrust into her simultaneously.

"Harder," she begged, her voice barely audible over the sound of their bodies colliding. They obliged, slamming into her with increased force, driving her to dizzying heights of ecstasy.

"Fuck, I can feel him inside you," Alexander growled, his eyes locked on Amelia's as he fucked her relentlessly. "Can you feel us both?"

"Y-yes," she stammered, her body quivering under their touch. "Don't stop."

"Good girl," William praised, his voice laced with lust. "Take us both, Amelia. Let us own every part of you."

As Amelia surrendered herself completely to the two men who had ignited her darkest fantasies, she knew that this moment – this wild, taboo encounter – would be forever seared into her mind, a testament to the depths of her own carnal desires and the power of surrendering to the forbidden.

Amelia lay on the rumpled sheets, a sheen of sweat glistening on her flushed skin as she panted softly. Alexander and William lounged on either side of her, their chests heaving in sync with hers, evidence of the recent passionate exertions they had shared.

"God, that was amazing," Amelia whispered, her voice husky from all the moans and cries she had released earlier. She turned her head to look at Alexander, his dark hair mussed and damp at the temples. He grinned at her, his eyes twinkling with mischief and satisfaction.

"Indeed, it was," Alexander agreed, his hand lazily tracing circles on Amelia's thigh, sending shivers up her spine.

William, ever the gentleman, draped one arm over Amelia's waist, pulling her closer to him. "I must say, I've never experienced anything quite like this before."

"Neither have I," Amelia confessed, feeling a blush creep up her cheeks despite her boldness throughout the night. The three of them laid there for a few moments longer, basking in the afterglow of their sexual adventures.

Finally, Amelia sighed, knowing they couldn't stay like this forever. "I suppose we should get dressed and part ways for the night."

"Unfortunately, you're right," Alexander conceded, pressing a lingering kiss to her shoulder before he rose from the bed, his naked form unabashedly on display as he began to collect his clothes. Amelia's gaze followed him appreciatively, her mind already reminiscing on the way his hands and lips had felt on her body.

William reluctantly disentangled himself from Amelia and started to dress as well. "But let's promise each other that this won't be the last time," he suggested, his voice low and full of desire.

"Agreed," Amelia murmured, watching as both men dressed themselves.

"Until next time, then," Alexander said, leaning down to give Amelia a parting kiss on the lips. She tasted the lingering heat of their passion and felt her heart race at the thought of meeting again.

"NEXT TIME," William echoed, pressing his own kiss to her forehead before they all left the room, returning to their respective homes with the memory of this night burning in their minds.

3

A couple of weeks later, Amelia received a letter from William, the handwriting elegant and precise. Her hands trembled as she unfolded the parchment, eager to see what he had written.

"Dearest Amelia and Alexander," the letter began, "I trust this letter finds you both well. I have been unable to stop thinking about our last encounter and find that my desire for another rendezvous grows stronger each day."

"Please meet me at the secret hideaway in the woods tomorrow night, where we can once again indulge in our passions without fear of discovery. The attached map will lead you there. I eagerly await our next adventure together. Yours always, William."

Amelia's breath hitched as she read the words, her mind already racing with thoughts of another steamy night with both men. She could hardly wait to be enveloped by their strong arms, their mouths leaving trails of fire across her skin, and their bodies moving in perfect harmony with hers.

"Until then," Amelia whispered, clutching the letter to her chest, anticipation coursing through her veins.

The moon cast a silvery glow over the secluded hideaway in the woods, where Amelia stood waiting. Her heart pounded with anticipation as she recalled the explicit instructions of William's letter. The rustling of leaves signaled the arrival of Alexander and William, their strong forms emerging from the shadows.

"Amelia," Alexander greeted her, his voice a sultry purr that sent shivers down her spine. "You look ravishing."

"Indeed," agreed William, his eyes dark and hungry as they devoured her figure. "We've been craving you since our last encounter."

"Likewise," Amelia confessed, her chest heaving with desire. "I've dreamt of this moment, of having both of you take me again."

"Then let us waste no more time," purred Alexander, closing the distance between them. He pulled Amelia into a searing kiss, his tongue exploring her mouth with wild abandon. At the same time, William's hands roamed her body, teasing her sensitive flesh through the thin fabric of her dress.

"Let's get you out of these clothes," growled William, his fingers deftly unfastening the buttons at the back of Amelia's gown. It pooled at her feet, revealing her naked form to the moonlight and the lustful gazes of the two men.

"Fuck, you're gorgeous," Alexander groaned, pressing himself against her, his erection straining against his pants. "We're going to have so much fun tonight."

"Please, don't keep me waiting," Amelia begged, her own arousal mounting as she glanced at the hardness in both men's trousers.

"Your wish is our command," William said, swiftly shedding his garments before guiding Amelia to the soft grass beneath a canopy of trees. Alexander followed suit, joining them moments later.

"Tonight, Amelia, you are our queen," declared Alexander. "We'll worship every inch of you until you can't take anymore."

"Please," Amelia gasped, her body craving the sensation of being filled by both men's throbbing cocks.

"Your pleasure is our priority," murmured William, leaning in to capture her lips in a heated kiss while Alexander moved his lips down to her dripping pussy.

Alexander's skilled tongue danced along her folds, eliciting a moan of pure ecstasy from Amelia's lips. The sensation of his mouth on her sensitive bud sent waves of pleasure coursing through her body. Meanwhile, William positioned himself behind her, teasing her entrance with the head of his thick shaft.

"Are you ready, my love?" William whispered huskily into Amelia's ear, his breath hot against her skin.

"Yes," she gasped, arching her back in anticipation.

With a slow and deliberate thrust, William filled her completely, stretching her walls to accommodate his size. A cry of pleasure escaped Amelia's lips as he began to move within her, his rhythmic thrusts sending shockwaves of bliss through her body.

Alexander continued his erotic ministrations with his tongue, alternating between gentle licks and flicks against her clit and plunging deeper into her core. The combination of Alexander's oral expertise and the deliciously deep strokes from William had Amelia teetering on the edge of ecstasy. Her body writhed beneath their touch, every nerve ending on fire with pleasure.

"Harder," she moaned, her voice a desperate plea for more. "Don't hold back."

Alexander growled in response, his mouth leaving her slick folds to capture her lips in a searing kiss. At the same time, William's thrusts became more forceful, driving deeper into Amelia's depths.

The three of them moved in perfect harmony, a symphony of passion and desire. Amelia surrendered herself fully to the overwhelming pleasure, her body consumed by the intoxicating rhythm created by Alexander and William.

Their hands roamed over her trembling flesh, teasing her sensitive nipples and exploring every inch of her curves. The intensity built within her like a tidal wave, ready to crash and consume her whole.

And then it hit, a wave of ecstasy that tore through Amelia, sending her spiraling into an orgasm that shook her to the core. Her cries of pleasure echoed through the woods, mingling with the sounds of their own moans and groans of satisfaction. Her body convulsed in pleasure as she clung to the two men, her walls pulsating around William's throbbing length.

As her orgasm subsided, Amelia caught her breath, her body buzzing with the aftershocks of pleasure. Alexander positioned himself and thrust into her ass while William continued to move within her pussy, prolonging her bliss and pushing her to the edge once again.

They took turns pleasuring her, ensuring that no part of her went untouched. Alexander's lips claimed hers in another searing kiss while William's hands roamed over her body, his fingers skimming along every sensitive curve. The sensation was overwhelming, their combined efforts driving Amelia to new heights of pleasure.

"Oh god," she gasped, tugging at Alexander's hair as another wave of pleasure crashed over her. Her body clenched around William, milking him for all he was worth as he filled her with his hot release.

The three of them collapsed in a tangle of limbs, their bodies spent and satiated. Sweat glistened on their skin as they basked in the aftermath of their shared pleasure, the air thick with the scent of sex and satisfaction.

But it wasn't long before Amelia was ready to go again. This time she focused on Alexander first. As he lay on his back, she took his huge cock into her mouth and sucked it slowly until it started to get hard again. William sat back and watched while still catching his breath from before.

Alexander let out a low moan, "Keep going Amelia. That feels amazing."

Amelia continued to devour Alexander's cock and it quickly became hard as a rock.

As Amelia bobbed her head up and down, her tongue swirling around the sensitive tip of Alexander's shaft, William couldn't help but join in the excitement. He crawled closer, positioning himself behind Amelia, his own erection pressing against her.

"Turn around," William commanded, his voice low and seductive. Amelia released Alexander from her mouth and shifted on her hands and knees, displaying herself to him as an invitation.

Without hesitation, William plunged into her wetness from behind, causing a gasp of pleasure to escape her lips. The feeling of being filled by both men simultaneously sent waves of ecstasy coursing through her entire being.

Alexander groaned as Amelia took him back into her mouth, working him with eager determination while William thrust into her with a relentless pace. The three of them moved as one, creating a symphony of moans and groans that echoed through the night, lost in the depths of their passion.

Amelia's body trembled with pleasure as she was pushed to the brink of yet another orgasm. The pleasure intensified with each thrust and every stroke, building a fire within her that threatened to consume her entirely. Her moans grew louder, mingling with the grunts and groans of Alexander and William.

Sensing Amelia's nearing climax, William quickened his pace, plunging deeper into her with each thrust. Meanwhile, Alexander's cock grew impossibly hard in Amelia's mouth, his moans growing more desperate as he approached his own release.

Amelia's body tensed, her back arching as the pleasure surged through her. She was on the precipice of ecstasy, her senses heightened and every nerve ending aflame with desire. And then it happened—a tidal wave of pleasure crashed over her, tearing through her body like wildfire.

Her cries filled the night air as she convulsed, waves of pleasure crashing over her in relentless succession. The intensity of her orgasm rippled through Alexander and William, pushing them both to their limits.

"Tell us how much you want us, Amelia," commanded William, his rhythm in perfect sync with Alexander's.

"More! I need more!" Amelia moaned, her body writhing beneath William as he fucked her relentlessly, bringing her to the edge of climax again.

"Such a filthy little queen," Alexander growled, his pace quickening as Amelia's mouth clamped around him.

"Let yourself go, Amelia," urged William, his breathing ragged as he continued to drive into her. "We've got you."

With a final cry of ecstasy, Amelia surrendered to the waves of pleasure that engulfed her, her body convulsing as both men reached their own orgasms within her. They collapsed together in a tangle of limbs, Amelia panting heavily between the two men.

"Next time, we'll make you beg," promised Alexander, his fingers trailing over Amelia's sweat-slickened skin.

"Next time," she agreed, her voice husky with satisfaction as she drifted into a sated slumber in the arms of her lovers.

THE END

ABOUT THE AUTHOR

Eliza Finch is an author of short erotica set in either the Victorian or Regency eras.

Also check out:

The Bookshop of Desire on Amazon